MW00744045

CINDERELLA

By Brittany Candau

Illustrated by Cory Godbey

Based on the Screenplay by Chris Weitz

Executive Producer Tim Lewis

Produced by

Simon Kinberg

Allison Shearmur

David Barron

Directed by Kenneth Branagh

For C.P., my very own fairy godmother
—B.C.

For Courtney, my little sister and princess
—C.G.

Printed in the United States of America · First Hardcover Edition, January 2015   3 5 7 9 10 8 6 4 2   ISBN 978-1-4847-2360-9
F322-8368-0-15030
Library of Congress Control Number: 2014946145
For more Disney Press fun, visit www.disneybooks.com
For more *Cinderella* fun, visit www.disney.com/cinderella

ONCE there was a girl named Ella,
a sweet and imaginative child.
She loved to care for beast and bird
and roam the meadows wild.

Ella's father taught her to dance and read.
She believed in magic thanks to her mother.
They all thought themselves quite lucky
to live happily and to love one another.

For many years their home
was filled with laughter and with light.
But tragedy can strike any land,
and here it came one warm spring night.

Poor Ella's mother grew quite ill.
She would soon leave this world behind.
Holding Ella very close, she said,
"Have courage and be kind."

Ella swore to keep this promise,
sad and scared though she might be.
She tried to cheer up her dear father
and welcome her new stepfamily.

Drisella thought herself fine and clever.
Anastasia was rude and vain.
Still, neither was as bitter or petty
as their mother, Lady Tremaine.

Ella's father had to travel
to pay off his new wife's debt.
Ella promised to be patient,
to be happy, and not to fret.

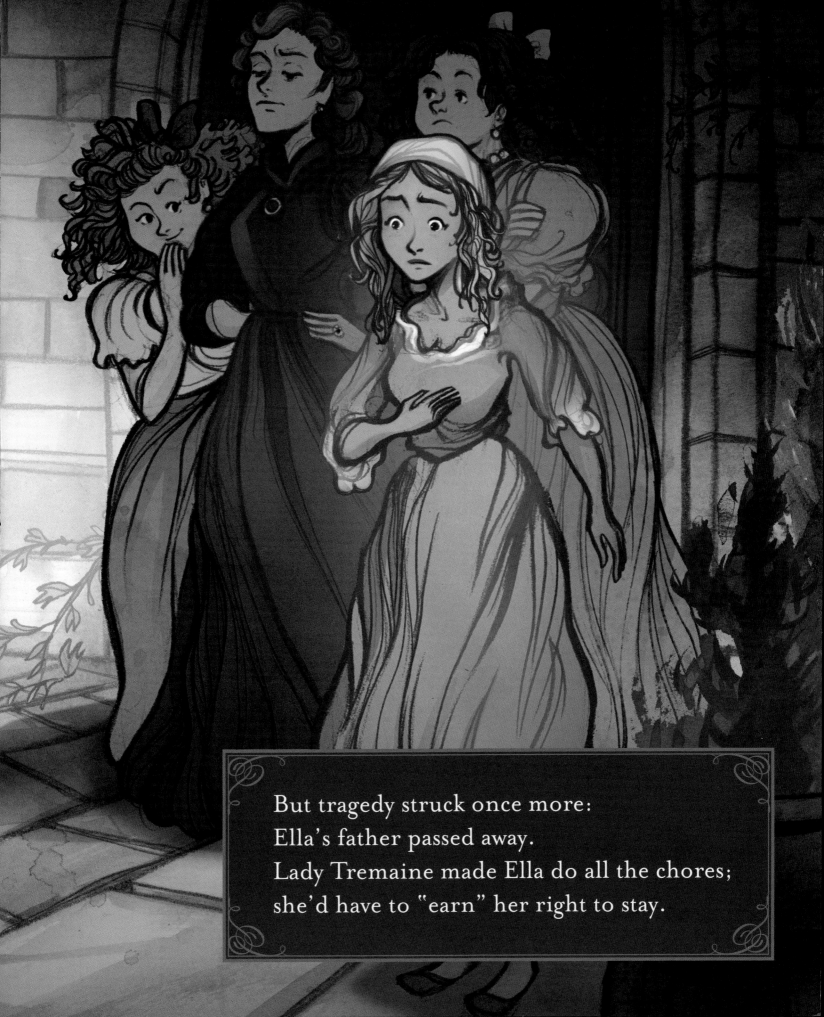

But tragedy struck once more:
Ella's father passed away.
Lady Tremaine made Ella do all the chores;
she'd have to "earn" her right to stay.

Now a servant in her home,
Ella tried to keep the peace.
Her parents were there in spirit, of course,
so her love for the house would never cease.

Yet her stepfamily's cruelty grew and grew.
She was taunted by Anastasia and Drisella.
And when she fell asleep near the fire,
they started to call her Cinderella.

Ella rode into the forest
to take strength and solace from the wild.
She breathed in the fresh cool air,
petted her horse's mane, and smiled.

Then, stumbling up on a group of hunters,
A mighty stag Ella did save.
And she met a sweet young man named Kit,
who was impressed by one so kind and brave.

Kit was really the prince,
but he did not share this fact.
He was afraid how this would change things,
afraid of how the maiden might react.

When Kit returned to the palace,
he knew his heart was won.
He couldn't forget her words:
*"Just because it's done, doesn't mean
it's what should be done."*

Later, in the market,
Ella heard a royal decree.
Every maiden was invited to the prince's ball,
noble or commoner, whichever she might be.

A chance for a night away!
A chance to forget her woe!
Ella would mend her mother's old dress,
late each evening she would sew.

At last, the night of the ball arrived,
and Ella put on her mother's gown.
But her stepfamily, ever jealous,
ripped and tore it down.

As the Tremaines left in their coach,
a beggar woman did appear.
Ella offered her bread and milk,
smiling kindly through her tears.

Suddenly, the woman transformed
into the face and dress of another.
For this new creature was actually
Ella's fairy godmother!

The Fairy Godmother turned pumpkin
into carriage,
mice into horses tall;
her magic would help sweet Ella
to attend the royal ball.

A darting lizard became a footman,
Ella's rags, a gown anew.
The Fairy Godmother made glass slippers,
for she knew the importance of a shoe.

The spell would end at midnight,
but Ella did not mind.
It would be a splendid evening,
and there was a friend she hoped to find.

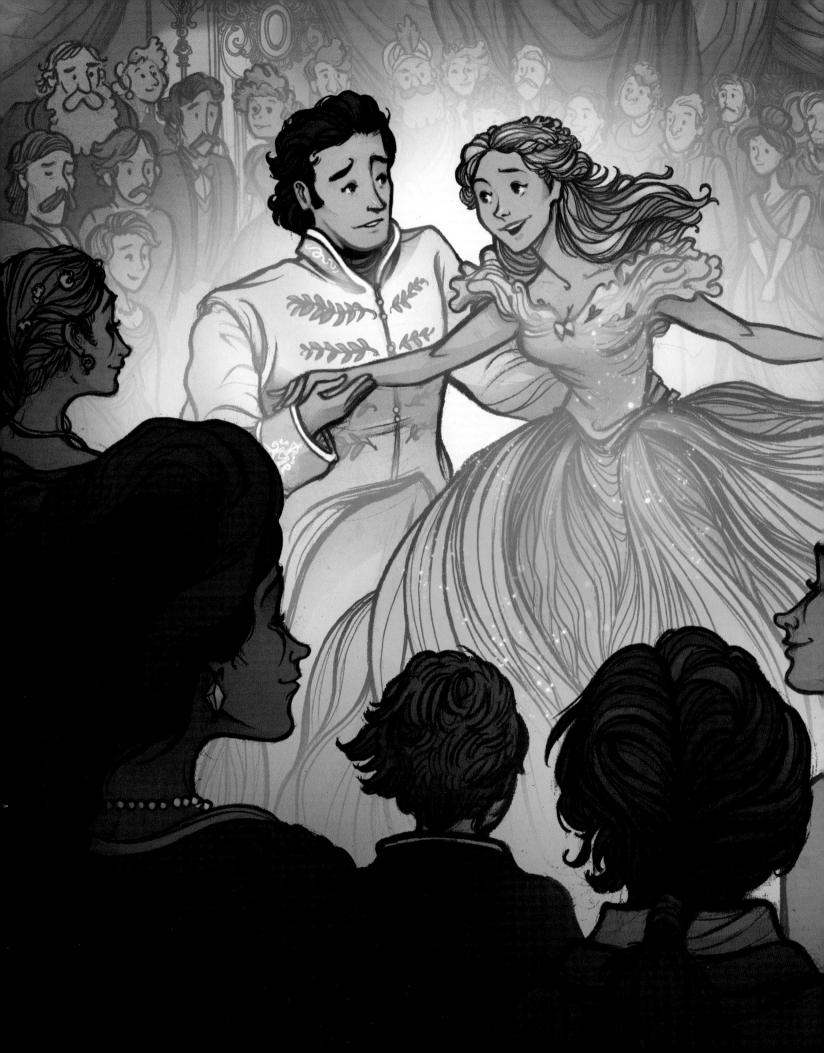

And lo, she spotted Kit in the ballroom!
They danced while all the guests stared.
But they only gazed at one another
as if no one else were there.

Ella and Kit spent a lovely evening,
touring the castle as their goal.
Ella learned Kit was the prince,
but also a dreamer, a kindred soul.

They explored a secret garden,
their spark of love growing into flame.
Yet Ella was afraid to tell Kit who she was.
She did not even share her name.

All too soon, the clock chimed midnight,
and Ella bade a hasty farewell.
One slipper slid off her foot,
but Ella left it, racing the sounding bell.

Suddenly, carriage became pumpkin
and Ella's gown returned to tatters.
She bravely faced the pursuing Duke
who thought a girl in rags could not matter.

The Grand Duke told Kit to forget the maiden.
But the sad prince wondered if she was all right.
He would declare his love for the girl in the glass shoes
with a royal proclamation that very night.

But dear Ella knew she had to have courage;
she would present her true self at the palace.
So Lady Tremaine smashed Ella's glass slipper,
and locked her in the attic with rage and malice.

The prince would not give up hope
of finding the one who'd disappeared.
He decided to try the slipper left on the steps
on every maiden, far and near.

Upon leaving the final cottage,
Kit heard the sound of singing sweet.
He realized there was one last foot
that the slipper had yet to meet.

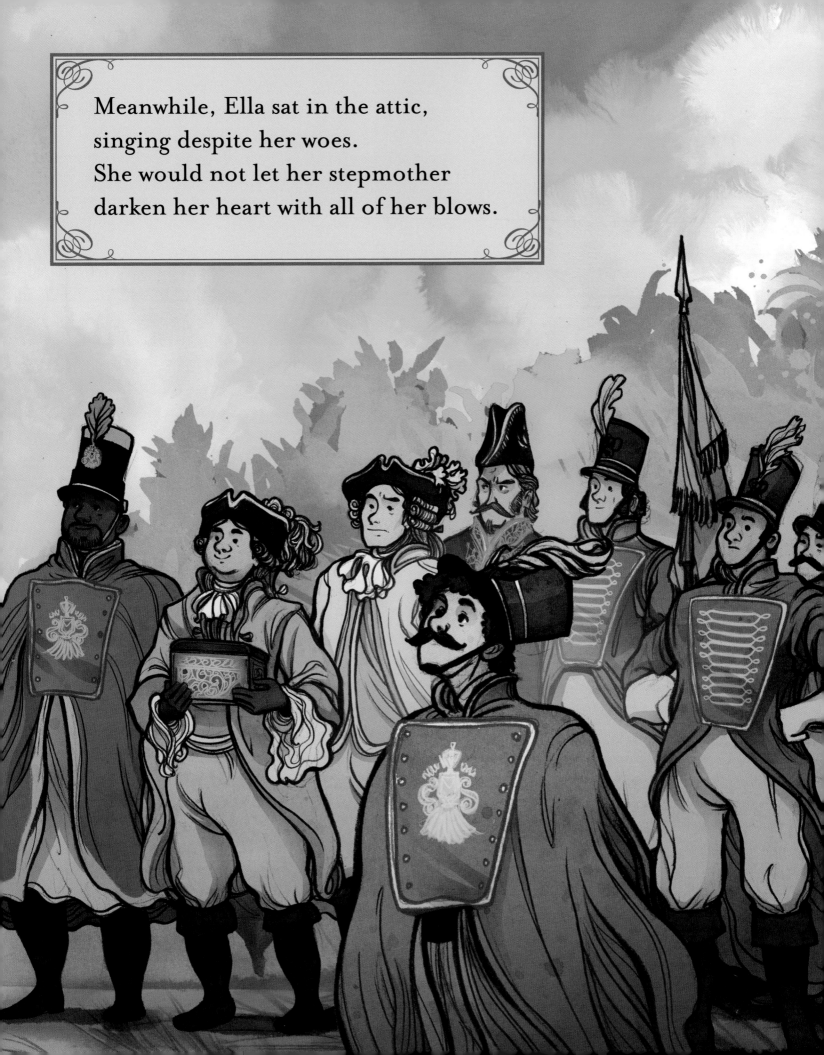

Meanwhile, Ella sat in the attic,
singing despite her woes.
She would not let her stepmother
darken her heart with all of her blows.

Kit ordered his captain to find the singer,
much to Lady Tremaine's dismay.
And when he saw Ella emerge,
he blinked happy tears away.

Ella told Kit the whole story,
asking him to accept her for her.
And smiling, Kit knelt down before her
and held out her lost glass slipper.

Soon Ella and Kit were wed.
They vowed to make the world better,
to have courage and be kind,
and to do it all together.